Hardback - ISBN: 978-1-923567-39-9
Paperback - ISBN: 978-1-923567-40-5
eBook - ISBN: 978-1-923567-41-2

Cover design by **Holly Symons**

For More, Please Visit

HollySymons.com.au

Chad's Guide to Coping When You're Probably Not a Goblin (But Still Have Goblin Feelings)

By Holly Symons

Dedication

To the feral weirdos.
To the emotionally traumatised.
To the ones who laugh too loud, feel too deep,
and overthink literally everything (even this
sentence).

To the goblins in disguise, the dragons in
hoodies, and the brave little squirrels carrying
acorns of unresolved emotional baggage.

You are not broken.
You are just having a really intense side quest.

This journal is for you.

With questionable qualifications and very real
affection,
— Chad, Goblin Life Coach

This journal is yours now. May it hold your mess, your magic, and your goblin breakthroughs.

With love, always—

THERAPY JOURNAL

Holly told me to tell you you're doing great. This is your journal now. Mess it up gloriously.

— **Chad,** who definitely forged Holly's

signature!

Introduction

Welcome to Your Chaos-Companion Journal
Hosted by Chad the Goblin Life Coach

Hi. I'm Chad.
I may or may not be legally qualified.
But I am emotionally available, and in the
Realmsverse, that counts for something.

You picked up this journal for a reason. Maybe
your brain is full of plot twists. Maybe your heart
is tired. Maybe you're just here for the jokes. All
are valid. All are welcome. (Even if you're a
squirrel. Especially if you're a squirrel.)

This isn't a typical therapy journal. There will be
emotional breakthroughs, sure—but also
doodles, snack-related metaphors, and advice
that sounds suspiciously like it was written by a
goblin with a psychology degree from the
University of Dramatic Coping.

Use this book however you need:
- Scribble in the margins.
- Cry on the pages.
- Laugh inappropriately.

- Take it one weird goblin day at a time.

You don't have to be a goblin to have goblin feelings.
But if you do, you're in very good company.

Let's do this.

— Chad
Officially Unofficial Life Coach of the Realmsverse

Part 1: Emotional Warm-Ups

*Because sometimes just surviving the week is worth a trophy. *

Prompt:

"Name three things that didn't destroy you this week. Go, you!"

1. ____

2. ____

3. ____

Reminder from Chad:

"Survival counts as a win. So does remembering to feed yourself."

Activity: Goblin Gratitude List

Write down the weirdest, smallest, or most chaotic things you're grateful for today.

(Examples: Soft socks, that one raccoon meme, surviving a social interaction.)

____

____

____

____

____

Doodle Zone:

"Draw your brain during a Monday."

(*Is it a storm? A scribble? A squirrel on caffeine? Let it out. *)

[Blank space for drawing]

Part 2: Anxiety, Chaos & Coping

Prompt 1:

"What does anxiety smell like? Now give it a ridiculous name."

Answer:

Prompt 2:

"Finish this sentence: 'If I disappear into the forest, I will need…'"

Answer:

Chad's Wisdom: "You are not too much. You're just high fantasy."

Part 3: Heartbreaks, Betrayals & Plot Twists

Prompt:

"Describe a betrayal. Now rewrite the ending as if you had a dragon."

Original betrayal:

____

____

____

Dragon-enhanced ending: -

____

____

____

____

____

Tangent Break:

Sir Tangent begins a heartfelt story about emotional pain, but halfway through, he starts describing a sandwich…

Then forgets the original point entirely and says, "Anyway, it had pickles."

Exercise: Goblin Grief Ritual

Step 1: Yell into a pillow.

Step 2: Eat a snack shaped like a coping mechanism (cookie, donut, possibly fruit if you're brave).

Step 3: Create a Goblin Grief Spell. Example:

"By the crumbs of the comfort snack, I declare this hurt less powerful than my dragon."

Step 4: Breathe. Cry if needed. Repeat as often as your story arc demands.

Part 4: Growth, Healing & Magic

Prompt:

"What version of you would a flower trust?"

Answer:

____

____

____

Affirmations from Gerald:

- You are soft and strong, like moss with boundaries.

- You deserve joy, even if today feels like a filler episode.

- You are not behind. You are blooming on Realmsverse time.

- You are doing better than your inner critic wants you to believe.

- Some days, showing up is enough. Today is one of those days.

Visualization:

"Your safe Realmsverse place. Draw it, describe it, or name it something inappropriate."

Draw: _________________________________

Describe: _________________________________

Name: _________________________________

Part 5: The Late-Night Panic Pages

Emergency Grounding Exercises:

1. Name 4 things you can touch.
2. Name 3 things you can hear.
3. Name 2 things you can smell.
4. Name 1 thing you can taste or are grateful for.

 The "Too Many Feelings" Checklist:

- ☐ I forgot to eat.

- ☐ I forgot to drink water.

- ☐ I forgot I'm not responsible for everyone else's feelings.

- ☐ I need a nap or a hug (possibly from a fictional dragon).

- ☐ I accidentally opened the memory vault again. Whoops.

- ☐ I survived anyway.

Goblin Breathing Guide:

"Inhale. Exhale. Scream into a cushion. Repeat."

Bonus: Flail like a dramatic bard if needed.

Part 6: Bonus Goblin Tools

Realmsverse Coping Cards:

- "Drink water. Not your enemies' tears."

- "Put the heavy thought down. You can come back to it later."

- "You're not stuck. You're just buffering."

- "When in doubt, ask: What would Chad do? (Then do the opposite.)"

"Plot Holes I've Survived" Worksheet:

• Plot Hole #1:

• Plot Hole #2:

• Plot Hole #3:

• What I learned (if anything): _

Fold-Out Realmsverse Mood Map (imagine this page unfolds magically):

- Angry Volcano

- Sad Swamp

- Meh Meadows

- Hopeful Hills

- Chad's Cottage of Questionable Advice

Chad's Official Certificate of Progress (Includes Glitter):

This certifies that _________________________
has made questionable but admirable progress in emotional self-discovery,

survived at least one mental plot twist and still showed up anyway. Gold stars, snacks, and glitter are hereby awarded.

Sample Prompt Page (Mock-up)

Prompt:

"Draw your inner chaos as a character. What's its name? Does it wear socks?"

Chad's Coaching Tip:

"Don't fight your chaos. Befriend it. Name it Steve and give it a hobby."

Daily Check-In:

☐ I expressed a feeling today

☐ I survived a plot twist

☐ I did not emotionally decapitate anyone

☐ I drank water, maybe?

Prompt Page – Draw Your Inner Chaos

Prompt:

"Draw your inner chaos as a character. What's its name? Does it wear socks?"

Name:

Socks? (Y/N):

Draw it here: ✏️

Chad's Coaching Tip:

"Don't fight your chaos. Befriend it. Name it Steve and give it a hobby."

Checkboxes:
- ☐ I expressed a feeling today
- ☐ I survived a plot twist
- ☐ I did not emotionally decapitate anyone
- ☐ I drank water, maybe?

Chad's Therapy Journal

Weekly Reflection Page

• What did you learn this week that surprised you?

• What tried to emotionally eat you alive and failed?

• What would Gerald say about your week?

Mood Tracker: Realmsverse Mood Map

Track your emotional journey through the Realms.
Mark your current location:

- Angry Volcano

- Sad Swamp

- Meh Meadows

- Hopeful Hills

- Feral Forest

- Chad's Cottage of Questionable Advice

Notes

Realmsverse Character Pep Talks

• Gerald: "You are more loved than your brain believes. Rest, roar, repeat."

• Loki: "You are chaos. Use it. Own it. Try not to blow up anything today."

• Chad: "You're doing great. I mean it. I read your thoughts. Some of them were snacks."

• Thor's Chicken: "*cluck cluck cluck! * (You're crushing it!)"

Creative Coping Pages

• Design Your Own Emotional Armour:

• If your anxiety were a potion, what's in it?

• Create a spell to summon peace (or snacks):

• Draw your brain with better Wi-Fi: ✏️

Letters You'll Never Send

• To someone who hurt you:

____

____

____

____

____

____

____

____

____

____

____

Notes

Write:

• To the younger you:

____

____

____

____

____

____

• To the villain in your story (plot twist, it's you):

____

____

____

____

____

____

Realmsverse Self-Care Quests

• Hydration Quest – collect 3 goblets of water today

• The Quest for Clean Laundry

• Summon Your Support Party (list 3 people or pets who get it):

1. _______________________________________

2. _______________________________________

3. _______________________________________

The Goblin Glossary

• Emo Gremlin Mode™: when your feelings sabotage your plans

• Feral Peace™: when you've accepted the chaos

• Snack Ritual: eating with emotional intent

Goblin Graduation Page

This certifies that _______________________________

has survived, thrived, and deeply scribbled their way through emotional goblinhood.

Awarded by Chad the Goblin Life Coach, with dubious authority and absolute affection.

Notes

30 Daily Chaos Pages – Chad's Therapy Journal

Day 1

Prompt:
What emotion is secretly running the show today? Give it a funny name.

Chad's Coaching Tip:
Name your emotions like pets. It's harder to fear something named Pickle.

Daily Check-In:

☐ I named my feelings

☐ I didn't spiral (much)

☐ I remembered I'm not doomed

Day 2

Prompt:
What would your goblin-self do right now if there were no consequences?

Notes

Chad's Coaching Tip:
Let your inner chaos goblin make a list. Then only
do the legal stuff.

Daily Check-In:

☐ I gave myself permission to want weird things

☐ I took one deep breath

☐ I stayed hydrated

Day 3

Prompt:
If today were a weather forecast for your feelings,
what would it be?

Chad's Coaching Tip:
Emotional thunderstorms pass. Just bring a
snack umbrella.

Daily Check-In:

☐ I checked in with myself

☐ I let something go

☐ I smiled (even sarcastically)

Notes

Day 4

Prompt:
What moment from today deserves a slow-motion replay with dramatic music?

Chad's Coaching Tip:
Celebrate the weird victories. Chad once earned a trophy for brushing his teeth.

Daily Check-In:

☐ I acknowledged a win

☐ I didn't judge myself too harshly

☐ I laughed

Day 5

Prompt:
Write a thank-you note to your past self for surviving something ridiculous.

Chad's Coaching Tip:
Your past self-did the best they could with weird goblin tools. Honor them.
Daily Check-In:

☐ I was kind to my past

☐ I didn't cringe at old memories (too much)

☐ I survived

Day 6

Prompt:
What emotion is secretly running the show today? Give it a funny name. (again, but new day energy)

Chad's Coaching Tip:
Name your emotions like pets. It's harder to fear something named Pickle.

Daily Check-In:

☐ I named my feelings

☐ I didn't spiral (much)

☐ I remembered I'm not doomed

Notes

Day 7

Prompt:
What moment from today deserves a slow-motion replay with dramatic music? (again, but new day energy)

Chad's Coaching Tip:
Celebrate the weird victories. Chad once earned a trophy for brushing his teeth.

Daily Check-In:

☐ I acknowledged a win

☐ I didn't judge myself too harshly

☐ I laughed

Extra Pages – Chad's Therapy Journal

Weekly Reflection Page

• What did you learn this week that surprised you?

____

____

____

____

____

____

____

____

____

____

Notes

• What tried to emotionally eat you alive and failed?

____

____

____

____

____

• What would Gerald say about your week?

____

____

____

____

____

Mood Tracker: Realmsverse Mood Map

Track your emotional journey through the Realms. Mark your current location:

- Angry Volcano

- Sad Swamp

- Meh Meadows

- Hopeful Hills

- Feral Forest

- Chad's Cottage of Questionable Advice

Realmsverse Character Pep Talks

• Gerald: "You are more loved than your brain believes. Rest, roar, repeat."

• Loki: "You are chaos. Use it. Own it. Try not to blow up anything today."

• Chad: "You're doing great. I mean it. I read your thoughts. Some of them were snacks."

Notes

• Thor's Chicken: "*cluck cluck cluck! * (You're crushing it!)"

Creative Coping Pages

• Design Your Own Emotional Armor:

Creative Coping Pages

• If your anxiety were a potion, what's in it?

Creative Coping Pages

- Create a spell to summon peace (or snacks):

Creative Coping Pages

• Draw your brain with better Wi-Fi: ✏️

Letters You'll Never Send

- To someone who hurt you:

Letters You'll Never Send

- To the villain in your story (plot twist, it's you):

Realmsverse Self-Care Quests

- Hydration Quest – collect 3 goblets of water today

Notes

The Quest for Clean Laundry

• Summon Your Support Party (list 3 people or pets who get it):

1.___________________________________

2.___________________________________

3.___________________________________

The Goblin Glossary

• Emo Gremlin Mode™: when your feelings sabotage your plans

• Feral Peace™: when you've accepted the chaos

• Snack Ritual: eating with emotional intent

Goblin Graduation Page

This certifies that _________________________

has survived, thrived, and deeply scribbled their way through emotional goblinhood.

Awarded by Chad the Goblin Life Coach, with dubious authority and absolute affection.

Notes

Day 8

Prompt:

What would your goblin self-do right now if there were no consequences? (again, but new day energy)

 Chad's Coaching Tip:

Let your inner chaos goblin make a list. Then only do the legal stuff.

Daily Check-In:

☐ I gave myself permission to want weird things

☐ I took one deep breath

☐ I stayed hydrated

Notes

Day 9

Prompt:

What moment from today deserves a slow-motion replay with dramatic music? (again, but new day energy)

Chad's Coaching Tip:

Celebrate the weird victories. Chad once earned a trophy for brushing his teeth.

Daily Check-In:

☐ I acknowledged a win

☐ I didn't judge myself too harshly

☐ I laughed

Notes

Day 10

Prompt:
If today were a weather forecast for your feelings, what would it be? (again, but new day energy)

Chad's Coaching Tip:
Emotional thunderstorms pass. Just bring a snack umbrella.

Daily Check-In:

☐ I checked in with myself

☐ I let something go

☐ I smiled (even sarcastically)

Notes

Day 11

Prompt:
What emotion is secretly running the show today? Give it a funny name. (again, but new day energy)

Chad's Coaching Tip:
Name your emotions like pets. It's harder to fear something named Pickle.

Daily Check-In:

☐ I named my feelings

☐ I didn't spiral (much)

☐ I remembered I'm not doomed

Notes

Day 12

Prompt:

What would your goblin self do right now if there were no consequences? (again, but new day energy) (again, but new day energy)

Chad's Coaching Tip:

Let your inner chaos goblin make a list. Then only do the legal stuff.

Daily Check-In:

☐ I acknowledged a win

☐ I didn't judge myself too harshly

☐ I laughed

Notes

Day 13

Prompt:

What moment from today deserves a slow-motion replay with dramatic music? (again, but new day energy) (again, but new day energy)

Chad's Coaching Tip:
Celebrate the weird victories. Chad once earned a trophy for brushing his teeth.

Daily Check-In:

☐ I acknowledged a win

☐ I didn't judge myself too harshly

☐ I laughed

Notes

Day 14

Prompt:
What would your goblin-self do right now if there were no consequences? (again, but new day energy)

Chad's Coaching Tip:
Let your inner chaos goblin make a list. Then only do the legal stuff.

Daily Check-In:

☐ I gave myself permission to want weird things

☐ I took one deep breath

☐ I stayed hydrated

Extra Pages – Chad's Therapy Journal

Weekly Reflection Page

- What did you learn this week that surprised you?

____

Notes

• What tried to emotionally eat you alive and failed?

• What would Gerald say about your week?

Mood Tracker: Realmsverse Mood Map

Track your emotional journey through the
Realms. Mark your current location:

- Angry Volcano

- Sad Swamp

- Meh Meadows

- Hopeful Hills

- Feral Forest

- Chad's Cottage of Questionable Advice

Realmsverse Character Pep Talks

• Gerald: "You are more loved than your brain
believes. Rest, roar, repeat."

• Loki: "You are chaos. Use it. Own it. Try not to
blow up anything today."

• Chad: "You're doing great. I mean it. I read your
thoughts. Some of them were snacks."

Notes

Notes

Summon Your Support Party (list 3 people or pets who get it):

1.___________________________________

2.___________________________________

3.___________________________________

The Goblin Glossary

• Emo Gremlin Mode™: when your feelings sabotage your plans

• Feral Peace™: when you've accepted the chaos

• Snack Ritual: eating with emotional intent

Goblin Graduation Page

This certifies that _______________________________

has survived, thrived, and deeply scribbled their way through emotional goblinhood.

Awarded by Chad the Goblin Life Coach, with dubious authority and absolute affection.

Notes

Day 15

Prompt:
What would your goblin self-do right now if there were no consequences? (again, but new day energy) (again, but new day energy) (again, but new day energy)

Chad's Coaching Tip:
Let your inner chaos goblin make a list. Then only do the legal stuff.

Daily Check-In:

☐ I gave myself permission to want weird things

☐ I took one deep breath

☐ I stayed hydrated

Notes

Day 16

Prompt:
What would your goblin self-do right now if there were no consequences? (again, but new day energy) (again, but new day energy) (again, but new day energy)

Chad's Coaching Tip:
Let your inner chaos goblin make a list. Then only do the legal stuff.

Daily Check-In:

☐ I gave myself permission to want weird things

☐ I took one deep breath

☐ I stayed hydrated

Notes

Day 17

Prompt:
What would your goblin self do right now if there were no consequences? (again, but new day energy) (again, but new day energy) (again, but new day energy)

Chad's Coaching Tip:
Let your inner chaos goblin make a list. Then only do the legal stuff.

Daily Check-In:

☐ I gave myself permission to want weird things

☐ I took one deep breath

☐ I stayed hydrated

Notes

Day 18

Prompt:

What would your goblin self do right now if there were no consequences? (again, but new day energy)

Chad's Coaching Tip:

Let your inner chaos goblin make a list. Then only do the legal stuff.

Daily Check-In:

☐ I gave myself permission to want weird things

☐ I took one deep breath

☐ I stayed hydrated

Notes

Day 19

Prompt:
What would your goblin-self do right now if there
were no consequences? (again, but new day
energy) (again, but new day energy)

Chad's Coaching Tip:
Let your inner chaos goblin make a list. Then only
do the legal stuff.

Daily Check-In:

☐ I gave myself permission to want weird things

☐ I took one deep breath

☐ I stayed hydrated

Notes

Day 20

Prompt:
What would your goblin-self do right now if there were no consequences? (again, but new day energy) (again, but new day energy) (again, but new day energy) (again, but new day energy)

Chad's Coaching Tip:
Let your inner chaos goblin make a list. Then only do the legal stuff.

Daily Check-In:

☐ I checked in with myself

☐ I let something go

☐ I smiled (even sarcastically)

Notes

Day 21

Prompt:
If today were a weather forecast for your feelings,
what would it be? (again, but new day energy)
(again, but new day energy)

Chad's Coaching Tip:
Emotional thunderstorms pass. Just bring a
snack umbrella.

Daily Check-In:

☐ I checked in with myself

☐ I let something go

☐ I smiled (even sarcastically)

Notes

Extra Pages – Chad's Therapy Journal

Weekly Reflection Page

- What did you learn this week that surprised you?

- What tried to emotionally eat you alive and failed?

- What would Gerald say about your week?

Mood Tracker: Realmsverse Mood Map

Track your emotional journey through the
Realms. Mark your current location:

- Angry Volcano

- Sad Swamp

- Meh Meadows

- Hopeful Hills

- Feral Forest

- Chad's Cottage of Questionable Advice

Notes

Realmsverse Character Pep Talks

• Gerald: "You are more loved than your brain believes. Rest, roar, repeat."

• Loki: "You are chaos. Use it. Own it. Try not to blow up anything today."

• Chad: "You're doing great. I mean it. I read your thoughts. Some of them were snacks."

• Thor's Chicken: "*cluck cluck cluck!* (You're crushing it!)"

Creative Coping Pages

- Design Your Own Emotional Armour:

- If your anxiety were a potion, what's in it?

- Create a spell to summon peace (or snacks):

- Draw your brain with better Wi-Fi: ✎

Letters You'll Never Send

- To someone who hurt you:

____

____

____

____

____

____

____

____

____

Notes

Realmsverse Self-Care Quests

• Hydration Quest – collect 3 goblets of water today

• The Quest for Clean Laundry

• Summon Your Support Party (list 3 people or pets who get it):

1. _______________________________________

2. _______________________________________

3. _______________________________________

The Goblin Glossary

• Emo Gremlin Mode™: when your feelings sabotage your plans

• Feral Peace™: when you've accepted the chaos

• Snack Ritual: eating with emotional intent

Goblin Graduation Page

This certifies that _________________________ has survived, thrived, and deeply scribbled their way through emotional goblinhood.

Awarded by Chad the Goblin Life Coach, with dubious authority and absolute affection.

Notes

Day 22

Prompt:

What moment from today deserves a slow-motion replay with dramatic music? (again, but new day energy) (again, but new day energy)

Chad's Coaching Tip:
Celebrate the weird victories. Chad once earned a trophy for brushing his teeth.

Daily Check-In:

☐ I acknowledged a win

☐ I didn't judge myself too harshly

☐ I laughed

Notes

Day 23

Prompt:
What would your goblin-self do right now if there were no consequences? (again, but new day energy) (again, but new day energy) (again, but new day energy) (again, but new day energy) (again, but new day energy)

Chad's Coaching Tip:
Let your inner chaos goblin make a list. Then only do the legal stuff.

Daily Check-In:

☐ I gave myself permission to want weird things

☐ I took one deep breath

☐ I stayed hydrated

Notes

Day 24

Prompt:
What emotion is secretly running the show today? Give it a funny name. (again, but new day energy) (again, but new day energy)

Chad's Coaching Tip:
Name your emotions like pets. It's harder to fear something named Pickle.

Daily Check-In:

☐ I named my feelings

☐ I didn't spiral (much)

☐ I remembered I'm not doomed

Notes

Day 25

Prompt:
If today were a weather forecast for your feelings,
what would it be? (again, but new day energy)
(again, but new day energy)

Chad's Coaching Tip:
Emotional thunderstorms pass. Just bring a
snack umbrella.

Daily Check-In:

☐ I checked in with myself

☐ I let something go

☐ I smiled (even sarcastically)

Notes

Day 26

Prompt:
What would your goblin self-do right now if there were no consequences? (again, but new day energy) (again, but new day energy) (again, but new day

 energy) (again, but new day energy)

Chad's Coaching Tip:
Let your inner chaos goblin make a list. Then only do the legal stuff.

Daily Check-In:

☐ I gave myself permission to want weird things

☐ I took one deep breath

☐ I stayed hydrated

Notes

Day 27

Prompt:
What would your goblin self-do right now if there were no consequences? (again, but new day energy) (again, but new day energy) (again, but new day energy) (again, but new day energy) (again, but new day energy) (again, but new day energy)

Chad's Coaching Tip:
Let your inner chaos goblin make a list. Then only do the legal stuff.

Daily Check-In:

☐ I gave myself permission to want weird things

☐ I took one deep breath

☐ I stayed hydrated

Notes

Day 28

Prompt:
What moment from today deserves a slow-motion replay with dramatic music? (again, but new day energy) (again, but new day energy) (again, but new day energy)

Chad's Coaching Tip:
Celebrate the weird victories. Chad once earned a trophy for brushing his teeth.

Daily Check-In:

☐ I acknowledged a win

☐ I didn't judge myself too harshly

☐ I laughed

Notes

Extra Pages – Chad's Therapy Journal

Weekly Reflection Page

- What did you learn this week that surprised you?

- What tried to emotionally eat you alive and failed?

- What would Gerald say about your week?

Mood Tracker: Realmsverse Mood Map

Track your emotional journey through the Realms. Mark your current location:

- Angry Volcano

- Sad Swamp

- Meh Meadows

- Hopeful Hills

- Feral Forest

- Chad's Cottage of Questionable Advice

Realmsverse Character Pep Talks

• Gerald: "You are more loved than your brain believes. Rest, roar, repeat."

• Loki: "You are chaos. Use it. Own it. Try not to blow up anything today."

Notes

Day 29

Prompt:
What would your goblin-self do right now if there were no consequences? (again, but new day energy) (again, but new day energy) (again, but new day energy) (again, but new day energy)

Chad's Coaching Tip:
Let your inner chaos goblin make a list. Then only do the legal stuff.

Daily Check-In:

☐ I gave myself permission to want weird things

☐ I took one deep breath

☐ I stayed hydrated

Notes

Day 30

Prompt:
What moment from today deserves a slow-motion replay with dramatic music? (again, but new day energy) (again, but new day energy)

Chad's Coaching Tip:
Celebrate the weird victories. Chad once earned a trophy for brushing his teeth.

Daily Check-In:

☐ I acknowledged a win

☐ I didn't judge myself too harshly

☐ I laughed

Notes

Day 30

Prompt:

What moment from today deserves a slow-motion replay with dramatic music? (again, but new day energy) (again, but new day energy)

Chad's Coaching Tip:

Celebrate the weird victories. Chad once earned a trophy for brushing his teeth.

Daily Check-In:

☐ I acknowledged a win

☐ I didn't judge myself too harshly

☐ I laughed

Notes

30-Day Chaos Check-In

So... How's Your Goblin Journey Going?

☑ Mini Reflection Prompts:

• What's the weirdest thing that helped you feel better this month?

- Which day made you feel the most unhinged (in a growth way)?

- Did you actually do the breathing exercises, or just scream into a pillow?

  ☐ Breathed like a champ
  ☐ Screamed like a bard
  ☐ Forgot both and ate a snack

Rate Your Realmsverse Experience:

☐ 0/10 – Still feral, send help

☐ 5/10 – Slightly more emotionally literate, still weird

☐ 10/10 – I *am* the goblin therapist now
 Bonus:

Give yourself a fictional medal for surviving 30 days of chaotic emotional work.

What's it called?

Notes

Notes

CHAD'S GUIDE TO COPING

CHAD'S THERAPY CRYSTALS

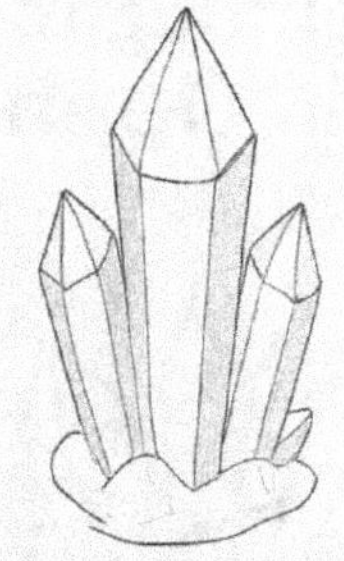

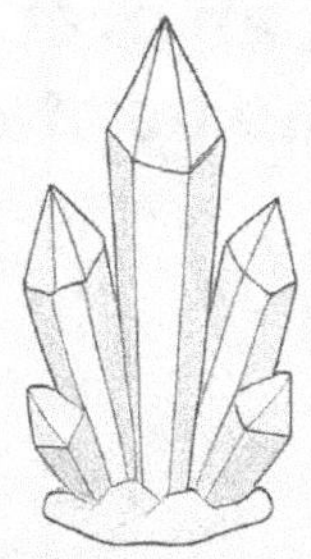

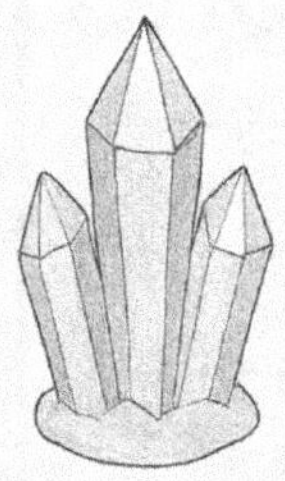

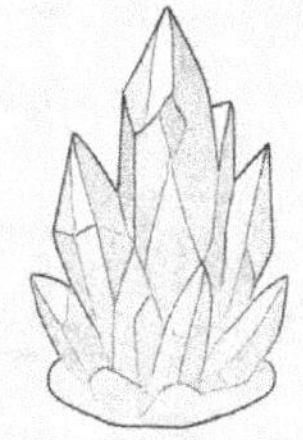

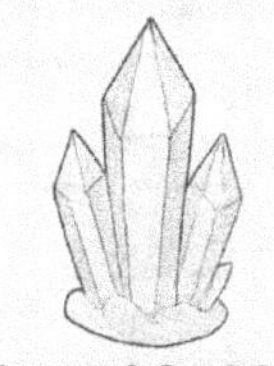

GOBLINITE
(FOR GETTING STARTED)

Colour an overwhelming to-do list with only
one box ticked: "Opened book."

☑ OPENED BOOK.

CRYNOCEROSE
(FOR FEELING WORSE)

Colour a mountain of tissues witah an emotionally-confused dragon

Prompt: Draw your meltdown. Label it *"growth."*

THINKING IS VALID. OVERTHINKING IS PERFORMANCE ART.

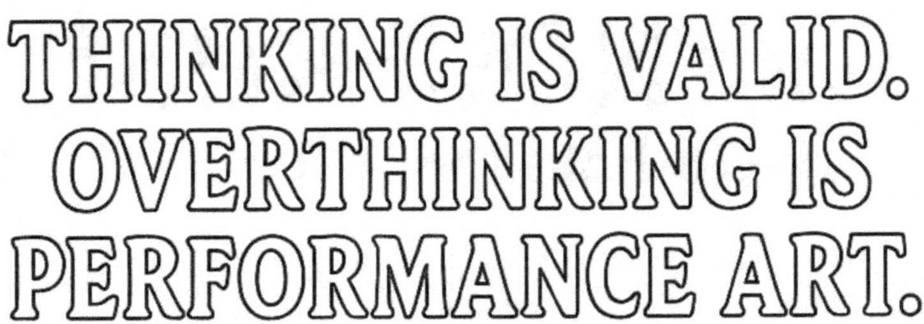

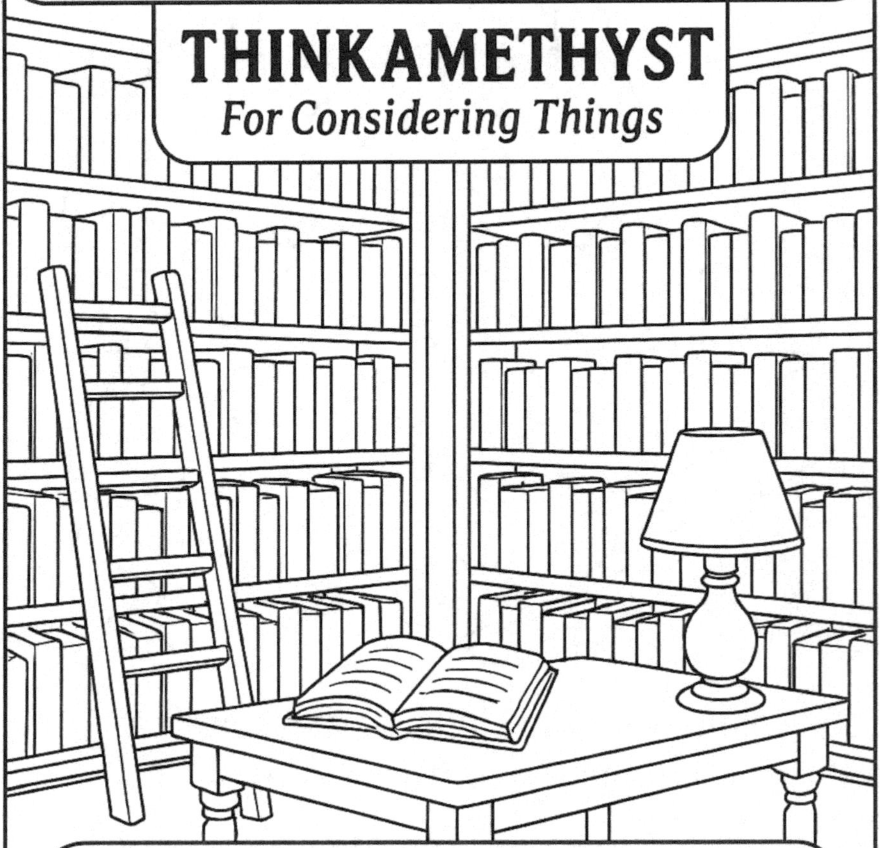

Colour a library full of unopened emotional books QUOTE: THINKING IS VALID. OVERTHINKING IS PERFOR-MATICALLY.

CHAD'S GUIDE
TO COPING

WRONGNITE
(FOR ACTIVE AVOIDANCE)

Colour a very detailed To-Don't List

Decorate the emotional broom closet where you stuff your feelings.

MOURNONITE

(FOR COPING)

"IT'S OKAY TO DO NOTHING.
BUT DO IT DRAMATICALLY

BLANKQUARTZ
(FOR CLEARING YOUR MIND)

Draw what's taking up too much space in your brain drawer.

BUZZBRITE
(For Energized Freakouts)

Draw the last time you spiraled—
but make it sparkly.

MEET
CHAD
the Goblin Life Coach

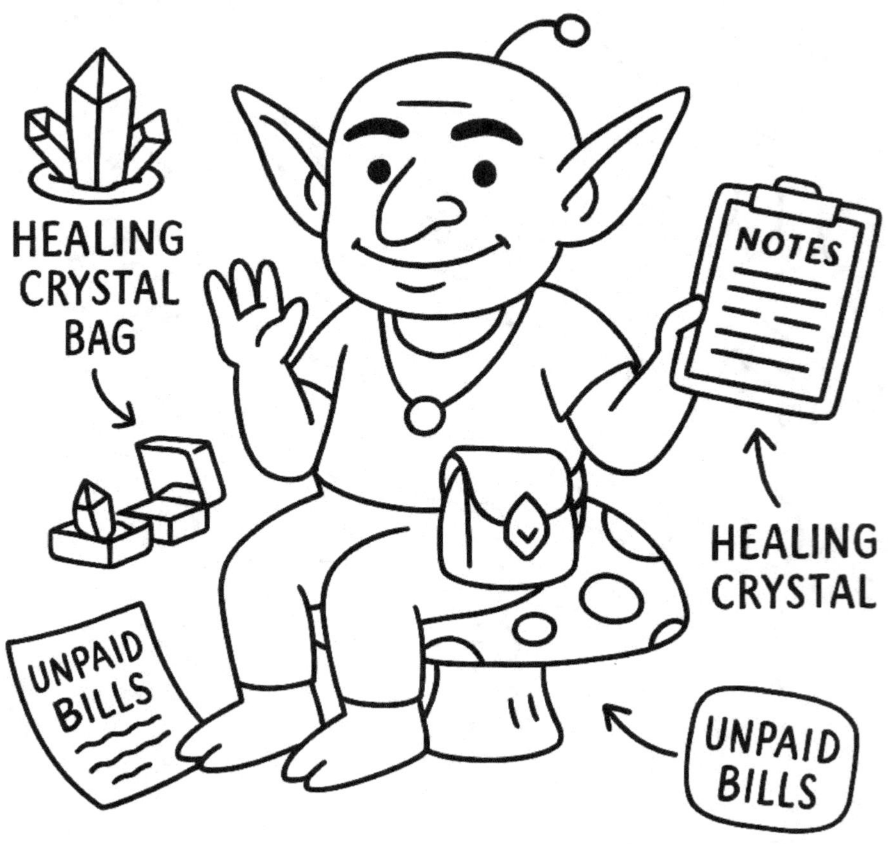

COLOR IN HIS MUSHROOM CHAIR,
HIS GLOWSTICK NECKLACE,
AND HIS UNPAID BILLS